Anonymous

Jesus in the Sacrament

Anonymous

Jesus in the Sacrament

Reprint of the original, first published in 1859.

1st Edition 2023 | ISBN: 978-3-37513-438-9

Verlag (Publisher): Salzwasser Verlag GmbH, Zeilweg 44, 60439 Frankfurt, Deutschland
Vertretungsberechtigt (Authorized to represent): E. Roepke, Zeilweg 44, 60439 Frankfurt, Deutschland
Druck (Print): Books on Demand GmbH, In de Tarpen 42, 22848 Norderstedt, Deutschland

JESUS

IN THE

SACRAMENT:

A

Little Manual for Benediction and Exposition,

The " Quarant' Ore," &c.

LONDON:

BURNS & LAMBERT, 17 PORTMAN STREET,

PORTMAN SQUARE.

1859.

[Price Twopence.]

Exposition and Benediction

OF THE

MOST HOLY SACRAMENT.

When the Priest opens the Tabernacle, and incenses the Blessed Sacrament, is sung the Hymn,

O salutaris Hostia,	O saving Victim, opening wide
Quæ cœli pandis ostium :	The gate of heav'n to man below !
Bella premunt hostilia,	Our foes press on from every side ;
Da robur, fer auxilium.	Thine aid supply, thy strength bestow.
Uni trinoque Domino	To thy great name be endless praise,
Sit sempiterna gloria,	Immortal Godhead, one in three !
Qui vitam sine termino	Oh, grant us endless length of days
Nobis donet in patria.	In our true native land with thee.
Amen.	Amen.

After which follows the Litany of the Blessed Virgin, *see* p. 41, *or some Psalm (the Psalm "* Quam dilecta," *will be found* p. 47), *or Antiphon, or Hymn appropriate to the Feast, or in honour of the Most Holy Sacrament. Here also are recited the corresponding Versicles and Prayers, as also any Prayer enjoined by the Bishop.*

If the Te Deum, p. 44, *be sung, the persons present stand until the words* Te ergo, quæsumus (We pray thee, therefore), *when they kneel.*

Then is sung the Hymn Tantum ergo Sacramentum, *all present making a profound inclination (not prostration) while the words* Veneremur cernui *are being said.*

Tantum ergo Sacramentum	Down in adoration falling,
Veneremur cernui :	Lo ! the sacred host we hail ;
Et antiquum documentum	Lo ! o'er ancient forms depart-
Novo cedat ritui ;	ing,
Præstet fides supplementum	Newer rites of grace prevail ;
Sensuum defectui.	Faith for all defects supplying
	Where the feeble senses fail.

Genitori, Genitoque
Laus et jubilatio,
Salus, honor, virtus quoque
Sit et benedictio:
Procedenti ab utroque
Compar sit laudatio.

To the everlasting Father,
And the Son who reigns on
high, [ing
With the Holy Ghost proceed-
Forth from each eternally,
Be salvation, honour, blessing,
Might and endless majesty!

Then are sung the following Versicle and Prayer.

℣. Panem de cœlo præstitisti eis. [Alleluia.]

℣. Thou didst give them bread from heaven. [Alleluia.]

℟. Omne delectamentum in se habentem. [Alleluia.]

℟. Containing in itself all sweetness. [Alleluia.]

Alleluia *is said in Paschal time, and during the Octave of* Corpus Christi.

Oremus.

Deus, qui nobis sub sacramento mirabili Passionis tuæ memoriam reliquisti; tribue, quæsumus, ita nos Corporis et Sanguinis tui sacra mysteria venerari, ut redemptionis tui fructum in nobis jugiter sentiamus. Qui vivis et regnas in sæcula sæculorum. Amen.

Let us pray.

O God, who, under a wonderful Sacrament, hast left us a memorial of thy Passion: grant us, we beseech thee, so to venerate the sacred mysteries of thy body and blood, that we may ever feel within us the fruit of thy redemption. Who livest, &c. Amen.

𝔙isits

TO

THE MOST HOLY SACRAMENT.

A Prayer for the Benediction of the Most Holy Sacrament.

O divine Redeemer of our souls, who of thy great goodness hast been pleased to leave us thy precious body and blood in the blessed Sacrament of the Altar, I adore thee with the most profound reverence. I humbly thank thee for all the favours thou hast bestowed upon us, especially for the institution of this most holy Sacrament. And as thou art the source of every blessing, I entreat thee to pour down thy benediction this day upon us, and upon all those for whom we offer up our prayers. And that nothing may interrupt the course of thy blessing, I beseech thee to banish from my heart all that displeases thee: pardon me my sins, O my God, since I sincerely detest them for love of thee; purify my heart, sanctify my soul, bestow on me a blessing like that which thou didst grant to thy disciples at thy ascension into heaven; grant me a blessing that may change, consecrate, and unite me perfectly to thee, and may fill me with thy Spirit, and be to me in this life a foretaste of those blessings which thou reservest for thy elect in heaven. All this I beg in the name of the Father, Son, and Holy Ghost. Amen.

Acts to be made at the beginning of each Visit to the Most Holy Sacrament.

My Lord Jesus Christ, who for the love which thou bearest to men dost remain day and night in this Sacrament, full of mercy and of love, inviting, expecting, receiving all them who come to visit thee, I believe that thou art present in the blessed Sacrament of the Altar. I adore thee, confessing my own misery and nothingness, and I thank thee for all the mercies which thou hast bestowed upon me, especially for having given me thyself in this Sacrament, for having given me thy most holy Mother Mary for my advocate, and for having called me to visit thee at this time. I salute thy most loving heart, and I desire to do so for three ends: 1, In thanksgiving for this great gift; 2, To atone for all the injuries thou hast received from thy enemies in this Sacrament; 3, To adore thee in all places in which thou art least honoured and most neglected in the holy Sacrament. O my Jesus, I love thee with all my heart; I am sorry for having hitherto displeased thy infinite goodness; I resolve, with the assistance of thy grace, never more to offend thee; and at this moment, miserable as I am, I desire to consecrate my whole being to thee. I give thee my will, my affections, my desires, and all that I have. From this day forward do with me, and whatever belongs to me, what thou pleasest; I ask and desire only thy love, the gift of final perseverance, and the perfect accomplishment of thy holy will. I recommend to thee the souls in purgatory, particularly those who were most devout to the blessed Sacrament and to holy Mary; and I recommend to thee all poor sinners. Finally, my dear Saviour, I unite all my affections with those of thy most loving heart; and thus united, I offer them to thy eternal Father, and I beseech him in thy name, and for thy sake, to accept them. Amen.

An Act of Spiritual Communion.

I believe in thee, O my Jesus, present in the most holy Sacrament of the Altar; I love thee above all things; and I desire to receive thee into my soul. Since I cannot now receive thee sacramentally, come at least spiritually into my heart. I embrace thee and I unite myself to thee, as if thou wast already there. Oh, permit me not ever to be separated from thee

TWENTY ASPIRATIONS OF LOVE TO JESUS IN THE ADORABLE SACRAMENT OF THE ALTAR.[1]

1. *Go forth, ye daughters of Jerusalem, and see king Solomon in the diadem wherewith his mother crowned him in the day of his espousals* (Cant. iii. 11).

O daughters of grace, souls that love God, come forth from the darkness of the world, and behold Jesus your king crowned with thorns, with the diadem of insult and of sorrow, with which his mother, the impious synagogue, crowned him on the day of his espousals, on the day of his death, by which he espoused himself on the cross to our souls; come forth again and behold him, full of all mercy and love, coming to unite himself to you in this Sacrament of his love.

My beloved Jesus, it has, then, cost thee so much to unite thyself to our souls in this most sweet sacrament; thou hadst first to undergo so bitter and ignominious a death! Come, then, O Lord, hasten to unite thyself to my soul. It was once thy enemy by sin, but now thou wilt make it thy spouse by grace. Come, Jesus, my spouse; I resolve never more to betray thee, but to remain faithful to thee for ever; as a loving spouse, I desire only to think of and to please thee. I would love thee without reserve; I would be wholly thine.

2. *A bundle of myrrh is my beloved to me: he shall abide between my breasts* (Cant. i. 12).

The myrrh plant, when it is bruised, sends forth tears and waters of health. To give us his blood for our sanctification, our Jesus wished to shed the last drop of it through his painful wounds. Come, then, beloved "bundle of myrrh," my dearest Jesus, who, when I see thee wounded and bleeding on the cross, art to me an object

[1] These may be used in visits to the blessed Sacrament, and also before and after communion.

of sorrow and compassion. But, in receiving thee in this most divine Sacrament, thou art more pleasant to me than the choicest grapes to a man oppressed with thirst. " A cluster of cypress is my love to me in the vineyards of Engaddi" (*Cant.* i. 13). Oh, what joy and sweetness do I feel in knowing that I am about to receive thee, my Saviour, who didst offer thyself in sacrifice on the cross for my salvation ! " He shall abide between my breasts." Yes, my Jesus, thou shalt never again depart from me. I wish to love thee always, and to be for ever united to thee in the closest bonds. I will always belong to Jesus ; Jesus shall be for ever mine.

3. *While the king was at his repose, my spikenard sent forth the odour thereof* (Cant. i. 11).

When Jesus comes to dwell in a soul by holy communion, oh, how does she, by the light which this King of heaven brings with him, see and know her own vileness, and, like the spikenard, the most lowly of plants, confess that she is the basest of creatures ! What sweet odour does she, when thus humbled, send forth to her beloved King, who invites her to unite herself more and more closely to him !

My soul, if thou desirest that Jesus should dwell within thee, see how low and wretched thou art ; humble thyself by banishing all self-esteem, which makes Jesus depart from thee, and prevents him from coming to repose within thee. Come to me, my dear Redeemer, and, by thy divine light, make me to know my vileness, my misery, my nothingness ; that so thou mayest rest with delight in my soul, and never more be separated from me.

4. *Think of the Lord in goodness* (Wis. i. 1).

My soul, why art thou so fearful at the sight of the infinite goodness and love of thy God ? Why art thou distrustful ? Now that thou dost receive Jesus Christ within thee, see that you correspond to his love, cou-

fiding in the boundless goodness of thy God, who gives
himself entirely to thee. His judgments truly are ter-
rible, but only to the proud and obstinate. To the peni-
tent and humble, who wish to love and please him,
they are all mercy and love, because they spring from a
heart full of compassion and love. Such are the judgments of God, that the royal Psalmist, in meditating on
them, was filled with hope and joy. " In thy words I
have hoped exceedingly. Thy judgments are delightful
. . . . I remembered, O Lord, thy judgments of old, and
was comforted" (*Ps.* cxviii 43, 52). Truly, this great
God is too good and loving to them that seek him with
love. " The Lord is good . . . . to the soul that seeketh
him" (*Lam.* iii. 25). Oh, how good is God to all who
endeavour to conform their will to his divine will ! "How
good is God to them that are of a right heart" (*Ps.*
lxxii. 1). My God, my love, my hope, my all, I desire thee,
and I desire thee only, that I may love thee, please thee,
and always do thy holy will. Grant that I may find thee,
that I may please thee, and that I may never more aban-
don thee.

5. *The voice of my beloved knocking: open to me, my sister,
my love, my dove, my undefiled* (Cant. iii. 2).

Behold the voice of Jesus in the blessed Sacrament
to those that love and desire him. Open to me, he says,
O Christian soul, thy heart; I will enter there, and dwell
with thee. Thou shalt become my sister by likeness to
me ; my love, by the communication of my graces ; my
dove, by the gift of simplicity; my undefiled, by the gift
of purity which I shall bestow upon thee. The spouse
adds : " For my head is full of dew, and my locks of the
drops of the night" (*Cant.* v. 2). Consider, O my beloved, I have waited all the night of the life of sin, which
thou hast spent in the midst of darkness and errors.
Behold, instead of coming to chastise thee with scourges,
I come with celestial dew, to extinguish in thee all im-
pure affections, and to kindle within thee the divine fire

of my love. Come, then, O my beloved Jesus, and work within me all that thou dost desire. I renounce all other affections, that I may be entirely thine, and that thou mayest make me altogether conformed to thy holy will.

6. *Let my beloved come into his garden, and eat the fruit of his apple-trees* (Cant. v. 1).

This is the invitation of a devout soul to Jesus in the blessed Sacrament. Come, O my beloved, she says, into my heart, which was once unhappily not thine, but has now, through thy grace, returned to thee. "Come, and eat the fruit of thy apple-trees." Come, and taste in me the virtues which thou thyself dost bring with thee. Ah, Lord, for the honour of thy majesty, at least, purify my soul, adorn it, inflame it with thy love, make it beautiful in thine eyes, that so it may become a fit abode for thyself.

7. *My beloved is white and ruddy, chosen out of thousands* (Cant. v. 10).

Our beloved Jesus is all white by purity, and all ruddy by the flames of divine love. Immaculate Lamb, all on fire with love for me, when wilt thou make me like to thyself? When wilt thou make me as pure as thou art, O most chaste lily? When wilt thou inflame me with the love with which thou dost burn for me? O my God and my all, I renounce all love, and choose only thy most amiable love. Depart hence from me all creatures; I wish only for my God: for him do I desire to reserve my whole heart and all its affections.

8. *The goodness and kindness of God our Saviour appeared* (Tit. iii. 4).

God, in becoming flesh, shewed to the world the extent of his goodness to mankind; but in the most holy Sacrament he displays the tenderness of his love for souls. "Does it not," says St. Augustin, "seem a folly to say, Eat my flesh and drink my blood?" as Jesus said on the night before his Passion: "Take, and eat; this is my body." To shew you the ardour of my love for you, I desire that you should eat my very flesh. O holy faith! Who but Jesus could have thought of instituting a means of giving us his body for the food of our souls! Some of his disciples, when they heard this, exclaimed, "This is a hard saying; who can hear it?" (John vi. 61.) They refused to believe the words of Jesus Christ, and "walked no more with him." But his words are of faith.

In return for all he has done for us, what more does Jesus Christ ask of us but to love him? Ah, my most loving Jesus, what dost thou not promise and give to them that love thee? Thou dost promise them thy love: "I love them that love me." (Prov. viii. 17.) Thou dost promise to receive them, though they have turned their backs upon thee. "Turn to me, saith the Lord of Hosts, and I will turn to you." (Zac. i. 3.) Thou dost promise to bring with thee the Father and the Holy Ghost, and to dwell for ever in their souls. "He that loveth me shall be loved of my Father, and we will come to him, and make our abode with him." (John xiv. 21, 23.) What more couldst thou promise or give to induce men to love thee? Most loving Lord, I understand thee; thou dost wish to be loved even by me. I love thee with my whole heart; and if I do not love thee, teach me to love thee. Make me love thee, and to love thee supremely.

9. *My beloved is gone down to his garden . . . . to feed in his garden, and to gather lilies* (Cant. vi. 1).

Most sweet Saviour, Jesus, since thou dost descend from heaven to enter into my soul, make me, I beseech thee, by thy grace, to become thy garden, that thou mayest gather in my heart lilies and fruits pleasing in thine eyes. Forgive me wherein I have offended thee; receive me now that I am sorry for my sins, and desire to return to thee; bestow upon me that purity which thou desirest, give me strength to do thy will, infuse into my soul a true love of thee, and then I shall be pleasing in thy sight. I sacrifice to thee all my inclinations; I desire henceforth only to please thee.

10. *He is all lovely* (Cant. v. 16).

To the souls that love him as their spouse, Jesus is "all lovely," whether he chastises or consoles them, whether he is near to or at a distance from them; because he does all from love and from a desire to be loved. Treat me, then, O my Jesus, as thou pleasest; I will love thee, whether thou dost send me consolations or afflictions. I know that all proceeds from thy loving heart, and that all shall be for my greater good. "My heart is ready, O God, my heart is ready." My will is prepared to embrace all the arrangements of thy providence: "I will bless the Lord at all times." At all times, whether in prosperity or adversity, I wish to bless and love thee, O Lord my Creator. I, who have so often displeased by my sins, neither seek nor merit consolations from thee. I seek only thy pleasure; and if thou art satisfied, I will bear cheerfully every affliction. O my Jesus, whether far off or near, thou shalt be always lovely, always dear to me; whether thou dost comfort or afflict me, I will always love thee, I will always thank thee.

11. *Who is this that cometh up from the desert, flowing with delights, leaning upon her beloved !* (Cant. viii. 5.)

Ah, who are those souls who, though they live in this world, regard it as a desert, and, detached from visible things, live only to God, as if he alone existed? whom only they love and desire to please; and who, raising themselves above the earth, enjoy the delights imparted to those who seek God alone, and place in him all their hopes !

Who are these happy souls? Are they not those who frequently unite themselves by pure love to Jesus in the most holy Sacrament? O my God, I desire to be, by thy grace, one of these blessed souls, to be detached from all things, and to be wholly thine. Henceforth the world shall be to me as a desert, where I shall be disengaged from every creature, and think only of thee as if there were none other than thyself and me. In thee alone will I place all my confidence; thou shalt be the centre of my affections; thou alone, O my God, my beloved, art my hope, my love, my all.

12. *I found him whom my soul loveth; I held him, and I will not let him go* (Cant. iii. 4).

Such should be the language of every soul united to Jesus in the most holy Sacrament. Creatures, depart from me: I loved you once because I was blind; but I love you no longer, nor can I ever love you more. I have found one far more worthy of my love. I have within me my Jesus; he has enamoured my whole soul with his beauty; to this beloved one I have given my whole being. He has accepted me as his; therefore I am no longer my own. Creatures, farewell; I am not, and never shall be yours. I belong, and shall for ever belong, to Jesus. "I held him, and I will not let him go." I will henceforth embrace him with my love, and will never more permit him to leave me.

13. *Arise, O north wind; come, O south wind, blow through my garden, and let the aromatical spices thereof flow* (Cant. iv. 16).

Fly from me, O cold and noxious wind of earthly affections, and come, O sweet and warm breeze of holy love from the heart of Jesus in the holy Sacrament. Do thou alone blow through my whole soul, which Jesus has chosen for his garden of delights. Blow, and new and sweet odours of virtue shall flow from me. My Jesus, thou canst infuse this holy gift into my soul; from thee I hope for it, of thee I beg it.

14. *I have gathered my myrrh, with my aromatical spices* (Cant. v. 1).

The soul that has received Jesus in the holy Sacrament should be careful to gather myrrh, that she may be able to send forth the odours of those virtues which spring from mortification. " I have eaten the honeycomb with my honey." The soul that loves God alone is not content with the honeycomb without the honey. Hence she says to Jesus: Lord, thy consolations are not sufficient without thyself, who art the source of consolation; the fruits of love are not enough for me without thyself, who art the object of all my love. My Jesus, thou art sufficient for me. I am ready to renounce all consolations, provided I possess thee alone, my God, and my only good. I love thee, not to please myself, but to please thee, who dost wish to be loved by me, and dost merit all the love of all souls, whether in joy or in sorrow.

15. *Behold, I have graven thee in my hands; thy walls are always before my eyes* (Is. xlix. 16).

Behold the sweet and loving care of God for the souls whom he loves! That he may not forget them, he carries them graven in his very hands, and declares that a mother will sooner forget her child than he will forget a soul in the state of grace. " Can a woman forget her infant ? . . . . . . And if she should forget, yet will not I forget thee." (Is. xlix. 15.) " Thy walls are always before my eyes." His eyes are ever watching over the souls that love him, to defend them against all the assaults of the enemy. " Thou hast crowned us with the shield of thy good will." (Ps. v. 13.) Our good God surrounds us with the shield of his good will, and delivers us from all dangers. O my God, O infinite goodness, who dost love me above all others, and desire my welfare, I give myself up entirely to thee. If thou art with me, all else may fail me. Behold me, O my dear

Lord, ready and resolved to do whatever thou willest; to desire only what pleases thee. But help me, O Lord, or I shall do no good: teach me not only to know, but to do all that thou dost wish me to do. Grant, O eternal Father, that I may be able truly to say what thy beloved Son said when on earth: "I do always the things that please him." (John viii. 29.) This grace, O my God, I desire, I ask and hope for, through the merits of thy Son, and of most holy Mary.

16. *What is there that I ought to do more for my vineyard that I have not done to it?* (Is. v. 4.)

My soul, hear what your God says to you. What ought I to do more for you that I have not done? For your sake I became man. I, the eternal Word, was made flesh: I, the Lord of all things, took "the form of a servant." Like a worm, I was born in a stable; "I was as a worm and no man." I even died for you, and died on an infamous gibbet: "I was made obedient unto death, even the death of the cross." What more could I do for you? "Greater love than this no man hath, that a man lay down his life for his friends." (John xv. 13.) But my love has done still more. I not only died for you, but I have also instituted the holy Sacrament of the Altar, that I might give myself entirely to you for your spiritual food, and that I might ever abide among you. Tell me, what more ought I to do to gain your love?

My Lord and my Redeemer, thou hast just reason to upbraid me, and I know not what to answer. Thou hast been infinitely good to me, and I have been infinitely ungrateful to thee. I admire thy infinite goodness; I behold my own ingratitude, and I prostrate myself at thy feet, saying, My Jesus, have pity on me, have pity on me, who have repaid thy love with so much ingratitude. Take vengeance on me; punish me, but not by abandoning me; rather do thou chastise and convert me. Permit me not to live any longer ungrateful to thee;

grant that, through gratitude at least, I may love thee, and that before I die I may make some small return for thy love.

17. *Put me as a seal upon thy heart* (Cant. viii. 6).

Yes, beloved Jesus, I have consecrated my whole soul to thee, and it is but just that I place thee as a seal of love upon my heart, to close it against all other love, and to proclaim to all that my heart is thine, and that thou alone hast the rule over it. But, O my Lord, what canst thou expect from me without the help of thy grace? I can but give thee my poor heart, to be disposed of as thou pleasest. Behold, Lord, I give it to thee without reserve; I consecrate it and sacrifice it wholly to thy love. I beseech thee, leave not my heart any longer in my own hands; for if thou do, I fear I shall only rob thee of it again. O most loving God, O infinite love, since thou hast so many claims to my love, make me, I entreat thee, to love thee. I desire to love thee only in order that I may please thee. Thou who dost work so many wonders in order to come into my heart in this divine Sacrament, perform yet one miracle more: make me wholly thine, without reserve or division, so that I may say in life, in death, and for eternity, that thou art the sole Lord of my heart, and my only riches. "Thou art the God of my heart, and my portion for ever." (Ps. lxxii. 26.) Most holy Mary, my mother and my hope, assist me, and I shall certainly be heard. Amen.

18. *How lovely are thy tabernacles, O Lord of Hosts; my soul longeth and fainteth for the courts of the Lord* (Ps. lxxxiii. 2).

O my God, the palaces of the great and noble are considered by men of this world as the happiest and most desirable abodes; but for me, I can find no satisfying place of rest but in the sacred tabernacles where thou abidest. There I would fain remain all the days of my life; and when at a distance from thy sacred

courts, I feel as in a strange land; my soul pants
thy sacred presence, and I exclaim with David, " Bles
are they that dwell in thy house, O Lord; they ab
praise thee for ever and ever." O my God, when su
happiness is to be found in thy presence, why sho
men so often leave thee alone and neglected, while
palaces of earthly kings are crowded with attendan
Alas, they know not the blessedness of possessing the
nor the happiness which they lose by not approaching
thee. As for me, I resolve, O my Jesus, henceforth to
visit thee as often as possible in thy earthly temples, in
which thou vouchsafest to dwell: I will come to adore
thee, to praise thee, to lament my sins before thee, to
seek light and comfort in all my difficulties and dis-
tresses, until the day arrives when I shall behold thee in
thy heavenly temple unveiled, and when thou shalt receive me to thy love for ever.

19. *In that day there shall be a fountain open to the house
of David, and to the inhabitants of Jerusalem, for the
washing of the sinner* (Zach. xiii. 1).

Jesus, in the holy Sacrament, is the fountain foretold
by the prophet, which is open to all, and in which we
can, whenever we wish, wash our souls from the stains of
our daily sins. When a fault is committed, what more
efficacious remedy can there be than to have immediate
recourse to the holy Sacrament? My Jesus, I purpose
always to avail myself of this remedy; for I know that
the waters of this fountain not only cleanse my soul, but
also give me light and strength to avoid sin, and to
suffer with joy all crosses, and, at the same time, inflame
my heart with thy love. I know that for these ends thou
dost expect me to visit thee, and dost reward with so
many graces the visits of thy lovers. My Jesus, wash
me from all the faults which I have this day committed;
I am sorry for them, because they have displeased thee;
give me strength to avoid them for the future, and to love
thee ardently.

O my only and infinite good, I see that thou hast instituted this Sacrament, and that thou remainest on this altar to be loved by me. For this end thou hast given me a heart capable of loving thee. Why, then, am I so ungrateful as not to love thee, or to love thee so little? The love which thou dost bear me merits far greater love from me. Thou art an infinite God—I am a miserable worm. It would be very little for me to die, to be consumed for thee who hast died for my sake, and who dost offer thyself in sacrifice every day for the love of me. Thou dost deserve infinite love. I desire to love thee with my whole heart. Assist me, O my Jesus; help me to love thee, and to do all thou dost require of me.

20. *While we are in the body, we are absent from the Lord* (2 Cor. v. 6).

Souls who, in this life, love nothing but God, are like noble pilgrims, destined to be the eternal bride of the King of heaven; but while they now live far away without seeing him, they sigh to depart to the country of the blessed, where they know that their Spouse awaits them. They know, indeed, that their Beloved is ever present with them in the blessed Sacrament of the Altar, but he is, as it were, hidden by a veil, and does not shew himself. Or, rather, he is like the sun behind clouds, sending forth, from time to time, some ray of his splendour, but yet not displaying himself openly. These holy souls live, nevertheless, contented, uniting themselves to the will of the Lord, who chooses to keep them in exile, and far away from himself; but, with all this, they cannot but continually sigh to know him face to face, in order to be more inflamed with love towards him.

When to these souls, thus filled with love for God, there appears any ray of the divine goodness, and of the love which God bears them, they would be dissolved and fade away for desire of him; and though for them the sun is still hidden behind the clouds, and his fair face is covered by a veil, and their own eyes are bandaged, so that they cannot gaze on him face to face; yet what shall be their joy when the clouds shall disperse, and the gate open, and the covering shall be taken from their eyes, and the fair countenance of their Beloved shall appear without a veil, so that in the clear light of day they shall look upon his beauty, his goodness, his greatness, and the love which he bears to them!

O death, why dost thou so delay to come? If thou comest not, I cannot depart to behold my God. It is thou who must open to me the gate, that I may enter into the palace of my Lord. O blessed country, when will the day be here when I shall find myself beneath thy eternal tabernacles! O beloved of my soul, my Jesus, my treasure, my love, my all, when shall come that happy moment, when, leaving this earth, I shall see myself all united to thee! I deserve not this happiness, but the love which thou hast shewn me, and still more thy infinite goodness, make me hope that I shall be one day joined to those happy souls, who, being wholly united to thee, love thee, and will love thee with a perfect love through all eternity. O my Jesus, thou seest the alternative in which I am placed, of being either ever united to thee, or ever far from thee: have mercy upon me: thy blood is my hope; and thy intercession, O my mother Mary, is my comfort and my joy.

Prayer for our Country.

O Lord Jesus Christ, infinite goodness, who by the divine Sacrament of thy Body and Blood dost refresh, comfort, and nourish thy Church, and daily offerest thyself a sacrifice of praise and propitiation to the eternal Father; look graciously upon our beloved country, shut out from the sweet delights of this banquet; mercifully pardon all that hath been done or said, through impiety or ignorance, against these most holy mysteries in this land; inspire the minds of all men with faith and reverence for them, that they may become thy children, and be as olive plants round about thy table. Who livest and reignest world without end. Amen.

Final Prayer.

Vouchsafe, O Lord Jesus Christ, with the Father and the Holy Ghost, to pour down upon me thy most holy benediction, that I may be enabled always to love thee, and seek to accomplish thy divine will in all things; and grant, O bread of angels, that I may deserve to receive thee during life, to be comforted by thee in death, and to enjoy thee eternally in thy heavenly kingdom. Amen.

ACTS OF ADORATION BEFORE THE MOST HOLY SACRAMENT.

Hail, Salvation of the world, Word of the Father, holy Host, true Life, living Flesh, perfect Deity, true Man, Body of our Lord Jesus Christ; thou who didst form me from the dust of the earth, have mercy upon me a sinner. Amen.

Hail, most merciful Jesus, Son of God and of the Virgin Mary, who didst so love me as to be pleased to die for me, and to give thyself to me as my support, my sacrifice, and my reward; be thou, with the Father and the Holy Ghost, blessed by all and above all for ever.

I grieve for all my sins, purely because they have displeased thee, and I resign myself to thee, and annihilate myself before thee. Supply, O merciful Jesus, for all the imperfections of us thy people, for whom thou didst deign to die, through the merits of the most blessed Virgin Mary and of all the Saints, which I offer thee in union with thine own most sacred merits, to be represented before the eternal Father. O holy Father, look upon the face of thy Christ, and grant us the grace to know thee, to love thee, and to praise thee, together with thy beloved Son, and the Holy Spirit, now and for ever.

All my holy patrons, and thou first, O most blessed Mother of God, praise the Lord with me, and let us exalt his name for ever. Amen.

O Lord Jesus Christ, true God and man, I humbly adore and invoke thee, now present in the verity of thy flesh and blood, thy body and soul. Would that I could truly contemplate and know thee, that I could love, praise, and glorify thee, even as do the thousands of holy angels who contemplate thee with the highest joy, who know thee, love, praise, and glorify thee perfectly without weariness or interruption. All creatures justly celebrate with praise and thanksgiving that ardent love of thine by which thou didst offer thy innocent and precious body upon the altar of the cross, and didst so lovingly, so graciously, so affectionately leave us in this holy Sacrament the same body, living and immortal, as a remembrance of thy departure, and as a pledge of thine infinite love.

O my Jesus, fountain of inexhaustible benediction, thou who, before thou didst ascend glorious into heaven, didst bless thy apostles, oh, bless me also, and with thy benediction sanctify me. Bless my memory, that it may ever recollect thee; bless my intellect, that it may ever think of thee; bless my will, that it may never seek or desire that which shall displease thee. Bless my body and its actions; bless my heart and its affections. Bless me now and in the hour of my death; bless me in time and in eternity; and grant that thy most holy benediction may be to me the sweet pledge of eternal felicity. Bless also my brethren, the faithful, who unitedly adore thee in this blessed Sacrament; and may thy benediction be an augmentation of grace to the just, and an effectual call to repentance for all poor sinners.

———

Adorations to Jesus in the Blessed Sacrament.

1. I adore thee profoundly in thy Sacrament, O my Jesus; I acknowledge thee there as true God and true man; and I intend by this act of adoration to make amends for the coldness of so many Christians, who pass before thy churches, nay sometimes before thy tabernacle, where thou deignest to dwell at all hours in a loving impatience to communicate thyself to thy faithful, and yet never so much as salute thee, and by their indifference, shew themselves to be like the Jews in the desert, sick of this heavenly manna; and I offer thee the most precious Blood which thou didst shed from the wound of thy left foot in reparation for such hateful coldness, within which wound I repeat a thousand and a thousand times—

Blessed and praised every moment,

Be the most holy and most divine Sacrament!

Our Father. Hail Mary. Glory.

2. I adore thee profoundly, O my Jesus; I acknowledge thee present in the most holy Sacrament; and I intend by this act of adoration to make amends for the ingratitude of so many Christians, who see thee carried to the poor sick, to be their comfort in the great journey of eternity, and yet leave thee without escort, and scarcely deign to make an act of outward adoration to thee; and I offer thee in reparation for such coldness the most precious Blood which thou didst shed from the wound of thy right foot, within which I repeat a thousand and a thousand times—

Blessed and praised every moment,

Be the most holy and most divine Sacrament!

Our Father. Hail Mary. Glory.

3. I adore thee profoundly, O my Jesus, true Bread of eternal life; and I intend by this adoration to make compensation to thee for the many wounds which thy sacred Heart daily suffers in the profanation of churches, where thou condescendest to dwell under the sacramental species, to receive the love and adoration of thy faithful; and I offer thee in reparation for all these irreverences the most precious Blood which thou didst shed from the

wound of thy left hand, within which I repeat again and again—

Blessed and praised every moment,
Be the most holy and most divine Sacrament!
Our Father. Hail Mary. Glory.

4. I adore thee profoundly, O my Jesus, living Bread come down from heaven; and by this act of adoration I intend to make amends for the many irreverences which are daily committed by thy people when assisting at the holy Mass, in which, through excess of love, thou renewest the same sacrifice, though bloodless, which thou hadst already accomplished on Calvary for our salvation; and I offer thee in reparation for such great ingratitude the most precious Blood which thou didst shed from the wound of thy right hand, within which I unite my voice to those of the angels, who gather devoutly round thee, and say with them—

Blessed and praised every moment,
Be the most holy and most divine Sacrament!
Our Father. Hail Mary. Glory.

5. I adore thee profoundly, O my Jesus, true Victim of expiation for our sins, and I offer thee this act of adoration in compensation for the sacrilegious outrages which thou receivest from so many ungrateful Christians, who dare to approach and receive thee in the Communion with mortal sin upon their souls. In reparation for such abominable sacrileges, I offer thee the last drops of thy most precious Blood which thou didst shed from the wound of thy side, within which I come to adore thee, to bless thee, and to love thee, and to repeat with all the souls devoted to the most holy Sacrament—

Blessed and praised every moment,
Be the most holy and most divine Sacrament!
Our Father. Hail Mary. Glory.

Tantum ergo sacramentum, &c.
Panem de cœlo, &c.
Deus, qui nobis, &c.

Indulgences: 300 days for every recital: applicable to the dead.

The Crown or Chaplet of the Blessed Sacrament.

℣. Deus, in adjutorium. Gloria Patri.

The Chaplet consists of thirty-three aspirations, which may be used during the hour of adoration before the Blessed Sacrament. After each aspiration may be added a Pater noster, *and at the end of each decade a* Gloria Patri.

First Decade.—Acts of Faith, Hope, and Charity.

I. I believe, O my Jesus, thy divine word, that under this appearance of bread thou thyself art here present as thou art in heaven. *Pater noster.*

II. I believe that thou art the divine Son, eternally equal to the Father, that by the operation of the Holy Ghost thou didst take human flesh of the Blessed Virgin. *Pater.*

III. I believe that thou art the same Jesus who wast born of Mary ever Virgin, adored an Infant by thy angels, by the shepherds and the magi. *Pater,*

IV. I believe, O my Redeemer, here present in Sacrament, that thou art the same Jesus of Nazareth who didst heal the sick, and didst raise the dead, who for us didst suffer and die upon the Cross. *Pater.*

V. I believe, finally, that thou thyself, now sitting glorious at the right hand of thy Father in heaven, and there interceding for me, yet art verily present in this Sacrament, my nourishment on earth. *Pater.*

VI. O most loving Jesus, who in this Sacrament hast left me a pledge of future glory, I hope, through the merits of thy death and passion, to behold thee face to face in heaven. *Pater.*

VII. O Jesus, cause of our glorious resurrection, I hope, through the virtue of this divine food, wherewith thou nourishest me, to rise glorious into life eternal. *Pater.*

VIII. I love thee, O Jesus, who art perfect charity, who, in thy essence, art true God and true man, in whom are contained the treasures of the divinity, and all the

fulness of grace which descends to us upon this earth.
Pater.

IX. I love thee, dear Jesus, who, for love of me, hast made thyself like unto me; kindle within me the flame of sacred love which thou didst bring from heaven, that, loving thee, I may grow into thy likeness. *Pater.*

X. I love thee, O divine Jesus, my Lord and Master, because thou hast redeemed and freed me, poor slave of sin, with thy all-precious blood. Oh, of thy sweet mercy, grant that I may enjoy the full fruit of thy redemption. *Gloria Patri.*

Second Decade.—*Acts of Adoration.*

I. I adore thee, O living bread, descended from heaven for my spiritual food; give me grace worthily to receive thee in life and in death. *Pater.*

II. I adore thee, divine food of the strong; strengthen my weakness, that I may ever be constant and faithful to thy love. *Pater.*

III. I adore thee, O my Jesus, hidden beneath the sacramental veil; let my life be hidden, through thee, in God. *Pater.*

IV. I adore thee, great God, who art the only way; make me ever to walk in the path of thy precepts, and after thy shining example, that so I may arrive at eternal salvation. *Pater.*

V. I adore thee, O Jesus, true and spiritual life of all who love thee, give me grace to die to myself, and to live to thee alone, who didst die for the love of me. *Pater.*

VI. I adore thee, my dear Redeemer, truth ineffable; enliven, I beseech thee, and increase my faith, that it may be fruitful in good works. *Pater.*

VII. I adore thee, O Jesus, divine light of the world; illuminate my mind, that, knowing, I may love thee, and may come to enjoy thee eternally in heaven. *Pater.*

VIII. I adore thee, divine and loving Shepherd; draw to thyself this wounded sheep, that it may never more leave thy fold, to fall into the hands of the infernal wolf. *Pater,*

IX. I adore thee, divine Lamb, who, for the sins of the world, didst give thyself to be slain; grant that I may bear all my sufferings patiently for thy sake, in satisfaction for my sins. *Pater.*

X. I adore thee, O Jesus, King of glory, Judge of the living and the dead: make me on earth so to fear thy justice, that in heaven I may eternally sing thy mercy. *Gloria Patri.*

Third Decade.—Acts of Thanksgiving.

I. I thank thee, O Divine Redeemer, that, not content with having for our sakes come upon the earth, thou hast instituted this adorable Sacrament, that therein thou mightst remain with us unto the consummation of the world. *Pater.*

II. I thank thee, O glorious Jesus, that thou dost veil, beneath the eucharistic species, thy infinite majesty and beauty, which thy angels delight to behold, that so I might have courage to approach the throne of thy mercy. *Pater.*

III. I thank thee, O Jesus most loving, that, having made thyself my food, thou descendest upon this tongue, which so often has offended thee, and dost enter within this body, which, alas, has too often deserved to be visited with thy anger. *Pater.*

IV. I thank thee, my dear Saviour, that in this ineffable Sacrament thou unitest me to thee with so much love, that I therein live in thee, and thou in me. *Pater.*

V. I thank thee, O my Jesus, that, giving thyself to me in this blessed Sacrament, thou hast so enriched it with the treasures of thy love: that thou hast not, thou canst not, thou knowest not, what greater gift to give me. *Pater.*

VI. I thank thee, O my good Jesus, that not only thou art become my food, but also in this blessed Sacrament offerest thyself a continual sacrifice for my salvation, to thy eternal Father. *Pater.*

VII. I thank thee, divine Priest, for that every day thou dost sacrifice thyself upon our altars, in adoration and homage to the most Blessed Trinity, and dost supply for our poor and miserable adorations.   *Pater.*

VIII. I thank thee, O my Saviour, because, renewing in this daily sacrifice the very sacrifice of the cross offered on Calvary, thou dost satisfy the divine justice for us miserable sinners.   *Pater.*

IX. I thank thee, dear Jesus, that thou hast become the priceless Victim, to merit for me the fulness of celestial favours.   Awaken in me such trust that their abundance may ever more and more descend upon my soul. *Pater.*

X. I thank thee, my loving Saviour, that thou art immolated in thanksgiving to God for all his benefits, spiritual and temporal, which he has bestowed upon me, and which I yet hope to receive.   *Gloria Patri.*

Three final Aspirations.

I. Jesus, invisible and divine Head of thy spouse the Church, who, with thy blood, hast purified her from all stain, have mercy upon her visible head, N., upon all bishops and pastors (especially N. our own Bishop), and shed upon them thy holy Spirit, wherewith thy apostles and disciples were filled, that they may maintain thy holy faith pure and untouched, and may spread over the whole world the light of thy Gospel and of thy Catholic truth.   *Pater.*

II. O Jesus, King of kings, Lord of governors, by whom monarchs do reign, and from whom all earthly power comes, mercifully behold our princes, and those in authority; infuse into them the spirit of thy divine wisdom, clemency, and justice, so that they may be great with thee rather than on earth, and may enter with thee into thy heavenly kingdom.   *Pater.*

III. O Jesus, all merciful, who didst not will the death of a sinner, but that he should be converted, and rise to a spiritual life; triumph, I beseech thee, over the malice and hardness of all who obstinately offend thee, so that, acquiring thy grace in this world, they may become worthy of the glory of thy heavenly Paradise for all eternity.   *Gloria Patri.*

✠

LITANIES.

Litany of the Saints.

Ant. Ne reminiscaris, Domine, delicta nostra, vel parentum nostrorum; neque vindictam sumas de peccatis nostris.

Ant. Remember not, O Lord, our offences, nor those of our fathers; neither take thou vengeance of our sins.

Kyrie eleison.
Kyrie eleison.
Christe eleison.
Christe eleison.
Kyrie eleison.
Kyrie eleison.
Christe audi nos.
Christe exaudi nos.
Pater de cœlis Deus,
Fili Redemptor mundi Deus,
Spiritus Sancte Deus,
Sancta Trinitas, unus Deus,
Sancta Maria,
Sancta Dei Genitrix,
Sancta Virgo virginum,
Sancte Michael,
Sancte Gabriel,
Sancte Raphael,
Omnes sancti Angeli et Archangeli, *Orate, &c.*

Miserere nobis. Ora pro nobis.

Lord have mercy.
Lord have mercy.
Christ have mercy.
Christ have mercy.
Lord have mercy.
Lord have mercy.
Christ hear us.
Christ graciously hear us.
God the Father of heaven,
God the Son, Redeemer of the world,
God the Holy Ghost,
Holy Trinity, one God,
Holy Mary,
Holy Mother of God,
Holy Virgin of virgins,
St. Michael,
St. Gabriel,
St. Raphael,
All ye holy Angels and Archangels,

Have mercy, &c. Pray for us.

Omnes sancti beatorum Spi- All ye holy orders of
  rituum ordines, *Orate, &c.*   blessed Spirits,
Sancte Joannes Baptista, St. John Baptist,
  Ora, &c.
Sancte Joseph, *Ora, &c.* St. Joseph,
Omnes sancti Patriarchæ et All ye holy Patriarchs
  Prophetæ, *Orate, &c.*   and Prophets,
Sancte Petre, St. Peter,
Sancte Paule, St. Paul,
Sancte Andrea, St. Andrew,
Sancte Jacobe, St. James,
Sancte Joannes, St. John,
Sancte Thoma, St. Thomas,
Sancte Jacobe, St. James,
Sancte Philippe, St. Philip,
Sancte Bartholomæe, St. Bartholomew,
Sancte Matthæe, St. Matthew,
Sancte Simon, St. Simon,
Sancte Thaddæe, St. Thaddeus,
Sancte Matthia, St. Matthias,
Sancte Barnaba, St. Barnabus,
Sancte Luca, St. Luke,
Sancte Marce, St. Mark,
Omnes sancti Apostoli et All ye holy Apostles and
  Evangelistæ,   Evangelists,
Omnes sancti Discipuli All ye holy Disciples of
  Domini,   our Lord,
Omnes sancti Innocen- All ye holy Innocents,
  tes,
Sancte Stephane, *Ora, &c.* St. Stephen,
Sancte Laurenti, *Ora, &c.* St. Lawrence,
Sancte Vincenti, *Ora, &c.* St. Vincent,
Sancti Fabiane et Sebas- SS. Fabian and Sebas-
  tiane,   tian,
Sancti Joannes et Paule, SS. John and Paul,
Sancti Cosma et Damiane, SS. Cosmas and Damian,
Sancti Gervasi et Protasi, SS. Gervase and Protase,
Omnes sancti Martyres, All ye holy Martyrs,

Ora pro nobis.

Orate, &c.

Orate, &c.

Pray for us.

Sancte Sylvester,		St. Sylvester,	
Sancte Gregori,		St. Gregory,	
Sancte Ambrosi,	*Ora pro nobis.*	St. Ambrose,	
Sancte Augustine,		St. Augustine,	
Sancte Hieronyme,		St. Jerome,	
Sancte Martine,		St. Martin,	
Sancte Nicolae,		St. Nicholas,	

Omnes sancti Pontifices et Confessores, *Orate, &c.* — All ye holy Bishops and Confessors,

Omnes sancti Doctores, *Orate, &c.* — All ye holy Doctors,

Sancte Antoni,		St. Anthony,	
Sancte Benedicte,	*Ora pro nobis.*	St. Benedict,	
Sancte Bernarde,		St. Bernard,	
Sancte Dominice,		St. Dominic,	
Sancte Francisce,		St. Francis,	

Omnes sancti Sacerdotes et Levitæ, *Orate, &c.* — All ye holy Priests and Levites,

Omnes sancti Monachi et Eremitæ, *Orate, &c.* — All ye holy Monks and Hermits,

Sancta Maria Magdalena,		St. Mary Magdalene,	*Pray for us.*
Sancta Agatha,		St. Agatha,	
Sancta Lucia,	*Ora pro nobis.*	St. Lucy,	
Sancta Agnes,		St. Agnes,	
Sancta Cæcilia,		St. Cicily,	
Sancta Catharina,		St. Catherine,	
Sancta Anastasia,		St. Anastasia,	

Omnes sanctæ Virgines et Viduæ, *Orate, &c.* — All ye holy Virgins and Widows,

Omnes Sancti et Sanctæ Dei, — All ye holy men and women, Saints of God,

Intercedite pro nobis. — *Make intercession for us.*

Propitius esto, — Be merciful,

Parce nobis, Domine. — *Spare us, O Lord.*

Propitius esto, — Be merciful,

Exaudi nos, Domine. — *Graciously hear us, O Lord.*

Ab omni malo, } *Libera nos, Domine.* — From all evil, } *O Lord, deliver us.*
Ab omni peccato,
From all sin,

Ab ira tua,*

From thy wrath,*

A subitanea et improvisa morte,

From sudden and unlooked-for death,

Ab insidiis diaboli.

From the snares of the devil,

Ab ira, et odio, et omni mala voluntate,

From anger, and hatred, and every evil will,

A spiritu fornicationis,

From the spirit of fornication,

A fulgure et tempestate,

From lightning and tempest,

A morte perpetua,

From everlasting death,

Per mysterium sanctæ Incarnationis tuæ,

Through the mystery of thy holy Incarnation,

Per Adventum tuum,

Through thy Coming,

Per Nativitatem tuam,

Through thy Nativity,

Per Baptismum et sanctum Jejunium tuum,

Through thy Baptism and holy Fasting,

Per Crucem et Passionem tuam,

Through thy Cross and Passion,

Per Mortem et Sepulturam tuam,

Through thy Death and Burial,

Per sanctam Resurrectionem tuam,

Through thy holy Resurrection.

Per admirabilem Ascensionem tuam,

Through thine admirable Ascension,

Per adventum Spiritus Sancti Paracliti,

Through the coming of the Holy Ghost the Paraclete,

In die judicii,

In the day of judgment,

Peccatores,

We sinners,

Libera nos, Domine.

O Lord, deliver us.

---

* Here, for the Devotion of the Forty Hours, is inserted:

Ab imminentibus periculis,

From all dangers that threaten us,

A peste, fame, et bello,

From plague, famine, and war,

Te rogamus audi nos.

Beseech thee, hear us.

Ut nobis parcas,	That thou wouldst spare us,
Ut nobis indulgeas,	That thou wouldst pardon us,
Ut ad veram pœnitentiam nos perducere digneris,	That thou wouldst bring us to true penance,
Ut Ecclesiam tuam sanctam regere et conservare digneris.	That thou wouldst vouchsafe to govern and preserve thy holy Church.
Ut Domnum Apostolicum, et omnes ecclesiasticos ordines in sancta religione conservare digneris,	That thou wouldst vouchsafe to preserve our Apostolic Prelate, and all orders of the Church, in holy religion.
Ut inimicos sanctæ Ecclesiæ humiliare digneris,*	That thou wouldst vouchsafe to humble the enemies of holy Church.*
Ut regibus et principibus Christianis pacem et veram concordiam donare digneris,	That thou wouldst vouchsafe to give peace and true concord to Christian kings and princes,
Ut cuncto populo Christiano pacem et unitatem largiri digneris,	That thou wouldst vouchsafe to grant peace and unity to all Christian people,
Ut nosmetipsos in tuo sancto servitio confortare et conservare digneris,	That thou wouldst vouchsafe to confirm and preserve us in thy holy service,

Te rogamus audi nos.

We beseech thee, hear us.

---

* For the Devotion of the Forty Hours, insert :

Ut Turcarum, et hæreticorum conatus, reprimere et ad nihilum redigere digneris.

That thou wouldst vouchsafe to defeat the attempts of all Turks and heretics, and bring them to nought.

Ut mentes nostras ad coelestia desideria erigas,

Ut omnibus benefactoribus nostris sempiterna bona retribuas,

Ut animas nostras, fratrum, propinquorum, et benefactorum nostrorum ab æterna damnatione eripias,

Ut fructus tèrræ dare et conservare digneris,

Te rogamus audi nos.

Ut·omnibus fidelibus defunctis requiem æternam donare digneris,

Ut nos exaudire digneris,

Fili Dei,

Agnus Dei, qui tollis peccata mundi,

Parce nobis, Domine.

Agnus Dei, qui tollis peccata mundi,

Exaudi nos, Domine.

Agnus Dei, qui tollis peccata mundi,

Miserere nobis.

Christe audi nos.

Christe exaudi nos.

Kyrie eleison.

That thou wouldst lift up our minds tó heavenly desires,

That thou wouldst render eternal blessings to all our benefactors,

That thou wouldst deliver our souls, and the souls of our brethren, relations, and benefactors, · from eternal damnation,

That thou wouldst vouchsafe to give and preserve the fruits of the earth,

We beseech thee, hear us.

That thou wouldst vouchsafe to grant eternal rest to all the faithful departed,

That thou wouldst vouchsafe graciously to hear us,

Son of God,

Lamb of God, who takest away the sins of the world,

Spare us, O Lord.

Lamb of God, who takest away the sins of the world,

Graciously hear us, O Lord.

Lamb of God, who takest away the sins of .the world,

Have mercy on us.

Christ hear us.

Christ graciously hear us.

Lord have mercy.

Christe eleison.
Kyrie eleison.
　Pater noster (*secreto*).
　℣. Et ne nos inducas in tentationem.
　℞. Sed libera nos a malo.

Christ have mercy.
Lord have mercy.
　Our Father (*secretly*).
　℣. And lead us not into temptation.
　℞. But deliver us from evil.

Psalm lxix. *Deus in adjutorium.*

Deus in adjutorium meum intende: Domine, ad adjuvandum me festina.

Confundantur et revereantur: qui quærunt animam meam.

Avertantur retrorsum, et erubescant: qui volunt mihi mala.

Avertantur statim erubescentes, qui dicunt mihi: Euge, euge.

Exultent et lætentur in te omnes qui quærunt te: et dicant semper, Magnificetur Dominus; qui diligunt salutare tuum.

Ego vero egenus et pauper sum: Deus, adjuva me.

Adjutor meus et liberator meus es tu: Domine, ne moreris.

Gloria Patri, &c.
℣. Salvos fac servos tuos.

1 O God, come to my assistance: O Lord, make haste to help me.

2 Let them be confounded and ashamed: that seek after my soul.

3 Let them be turned backward, and blush for shame: that desire evils unto me.

4 Let them be straightway turned backward blushing for shame, that say unto me: 'Tis well, 'tis well.

5 Let all that seek thee be joyful and glad in thee: and let such as love thy salvation say alway, The Lord be magnified.

6 But I am needy and poor: O God, help thou me.

7 Thou art my helper and my deliverer: O Lord, make no long delay.

Glory be, &c.
℣. Save thy servants.

c

℞. Deus meus, sperantes in te.

℣. Esto nobis, Domine, turris fortitudinis.

℞. A facie inimici.

℣. Nihil proficiat inimicus in nobis.

℞. Et filius iniquitatis non apponat nocere nobis.

℣. Domine, non secundum peccata nostra facias nobis.

℞. Neque secundum iniquitates nostras retribuas nobis.

℣. Oremus pro Pontifice nostro, N.

℞. Dominus conservet eum, et vivificet eum, et beatum faciat eum in terra; et non tradat eum in animam inimicorum ejus.

℣. Oremus pro benefactoribus nostris.

℞. Retribuere dignare, Domine, omnibus nobis bona facientibus propter nomen tuum vitam æternam.

℣. Oremus pro fidelibus defunctis.

℞. Requiem æternam dona eis, Domine; et lux perpetua luceat eis.

℣. Requiescant in pace.

℞. Who hope in thee, O my God.

℣. Be unto us, O Lord, a tower of strength.

℞. From the face of the enemy.

℣. Let not the enemy prevail against us.

℞. Nor the son of iniquity approach to hurt us.

℣. O Lord, deal not with us according to our sins.

℞. Neither requite us according to our iniquities.

℣. Let us pray for our Sovereign Pontiff, N.

℞. The Lord preserve him and give him life, and make him blessed upon the earth; and deliver him not up to the will of his enemies.

℣. Let us pray for our benefactors.

℞. Vouchsafe, O Lord, for thy name's sake, to reward with eternal life all them that do us good. Amen.

℣. Let us pray for the faithful departed.

℞. Eternal rest give unto them, O Lord; and let perpetual light shine upon them.

℣. Let them rest in peace.

R℣. Amen.

℣. Pro fratribus nostris absentibus.

R℣. Salvos fac servos tuos, Deus meus, sperantes in te.

℣. Mitte eis, Domine, auxilium de sancto.

R℣. Et de Sion tuere eos.

℣. Domine, exaudi orationem meam.

R℣. Et clamor meus ad te veniat.

Oremus.*

R℣. Amen.

℣. For our absent brethren.

R℣. Save thy servants, who hope in thee, O my God.

℣. Send them help, O Lord, from the sanctuary,

R℣. And defend them out of Sion.

℣. O Lord, hear my prayer.

R℣. And let my cry come unto thee.

Let us pray.*

---

* For the Devotion of the Forty Hours the following Collects are used:

Deus, qui nobis sub sacramento mirabili Passionis tuæ memoriam reliquisti; tribue, quæsumus, ita nos Corporis et Sanguinis tui sacra mysteria venerari, ut redemptionis tui fructum in nobis jugiter sentiamus. Qui vivis et regnas in sæcula sæculorum. Amen.

O God, who, under a wonderful Sacrament, hast left us a memorial of thy Passion; grant us, we beseech thee, so to venerate the sacred mysteries of thy body and blood, that we may ever feel within us the fruit of thy redemption. Who livest, &c. Amen.

From Advent to Christmas.

Deus, qui de beatæ Mariæ Virginis utero Verbum tuum, angelo nuntiante, carnem suscipere voluisti; præsta supplicibus tuis, ut

O God, who wast pleased that thy Word, at the message of an angel, should take flesh in the womb of the blessed Virgin Mary;

Deus, cui proprium es misereri semper, et parcere: suscipe deprecationem nostram; ut nos, et omnes famulos tuos, quos delictorum catena constringit, miseratio tuæ pietatis clementer absolvat.

O God, whose property is always to have mercy and to spare, receive our humble petition; that we, and all thy servants who are bound by the chain of sins, may, by the compassion of thy goodness, mercifully be absolved.

Exaudi, quæsumus, Domine, supplicum preces, et confitentium tibi parce pec-

Graciously hear, we beseech thee, O Lord, the prayers of thy suppliants,

---

qui vere eam Genitricem Dei credimus, ejus apud te intercessionibus adjuvemur. Per eumdem Christum Dominum nostrum.

grant to us, thy humble servants, that, as we believe her to be truly the Mother of God, we may be assisted also by her intercessions with thee. Through the same Christ our Lord.

℟. Amen.

℟. Amen.

From Christmas to the Purification.

Deus, qui salutis æternæ, beatæ Mariæ virginitate fœcunda, humano generi præmia præstitisti; tribue, quæsumus, ut ipsam pro nobis intercedere sentiamus, per quam meruimus auctorem vitæ suscipere Dominum nostrum Jesum Christum Filium tuum. Qui tecum vivit et regnat in unitate Spiritus Sancti, Deus, per omnia sæcula sæculorum.

℟. Amen.

O God, who, by the fruitful virginity of blessed Mary, hast given to mankind the rewards of eternal salvation; grant, we beseech thee, that we may experience her intercession for us, through whom we have received the author of life, our Lord Jesus Christ thy Son. Who liveth and reigneth with thee in the unity of the Holy Ghost, God, world without end.

℟. Amen.

catis: ut pariter nobis indulgentiam tribuas benignus et pacem.

and forgive the sins of them that confess to thee; that, in thy bounty, thou mayest grant us both pardon and peace.

Ineffabilem nobis, Domine, misericordiam tuam clementer ostende: ut simul nos et a peccatis omnibus exuas, et a pœnis, quas pro his meremur, eripias.

Shew forth upon us, O Lord, in thy mercy, thy unspeakable loving kindness; that thou mayest both loose us from all our sins, and deliver us from the punishments which we deserve for them.

Deus, qui culpa offen-

O God, who by sin art

From the Purification to Advent.

Concede nos famulos tuos, quæsumus, Domine Deus, perpetua mentis et corporis sanitate gaudere; et gloriosa beatæ Mariæ semper Virginis intercessione, a præsenti liberari tristitia, et æterna perfrui lætitia.

Grant, we beseech thee, O Lord God, that we, thy servants, may enjoy perpetual health of mind and body; and by the intercession of the blessed Mary ever Virgin, may be delivered from present sorrow, and obtain eternal joy.

Then follows the Collect for the Pope, after which is said:

Deus, refugium nostrum et virtus, adesto piis Ecclesiæ tuæ precibus, auctor ipse pietatis; et præsta, ut quod fideliter petimus, efficaciter consequamur.

O God, our refuge and strength, who art the author of all piety, hearken unto the devout prayers of thy Church; and grant that what we ask faithfully we may obtain effectually.

Omnipotens, sempiterne Deus, in cujus manu sunt omnes potestates, et omnia

Almighty, everlasting God, in whose hand are all the powers and all the rights

deris, pœnitentia placaris: preces populi tui supplicantis propitius respice; et flagella tuæ iracundiæ, quæ pro peccatis nostris meremur, averte.

offended, and by penance pacified, mercifully regard the prayers of thy people making supplication to thee, and turn away the scourges of thine anger, which we deserve for our sins.

Omnipotens, sempiterne Deus, miserere famulo tuo Pontifici nostro N, et dirige eum secundum tuam clementiam in viam salutis æternæ: ut te donante tibi placita cupiat, et tota virtute perficiat.

Almighty, everlasting God, have mercy upon thy servant N, our Sovereign Pontiff, and direct him, according to thy clemency, into the way of everlasting salvation; that by thy grace he may both desire those things that are pleasing to thee, and perform them with all his strength.

Deus, a quo sancta desideria, recta consilia, et justa sunt opera: da servis

O God, from whom all holy desires, all right counsels, and all just works do

jura regnorum, respice in auxilium Christianorum, ut gentes paganorum et hæreticorum, quæ in sua feritate et fraude confidunt, dexteræ tuæ potentia conterantur.

of kingdoms, come to the assistance of thy Christian people, that all pagan and heretical nations, who trust in their own violence and fraud, may be broken by the might of thy right hand.

Then follows the last Collect, Omnipotens, sempiterne Deus, &c., Almighty, everlasting God, &c., *with the Versicles, except that, in the last response but one, &c., instead of the simple* Amen, *is said,*

℞. Et custodiat nos semper. Amen.

℞. And ever preserve us. Amen.

tuis illam, quam mundus dare non potest, pacem ; ut et corda nostra mandatis tuis dedita, et hostium sublata formidine, tempora sint tua protectione tranquilla.

Ure igne Sancti Spiritus renes nostros et cor nostrum, Domine: ut tibi casto corpore serviamus, et mundo corde placeamus.

Fidelium Deus omnium Conditor et Redemptor, animabus famulorum famularumque tuarum remissionem cunctorum tribue peccatorum : ut indulgentiam, quam semper optaverunt, piis supplicationibus consequantur.

Actiones nostras, quæsumus, Domine, aspirando præveni, et adjuvando prosequere : ut cuncta nostra oratio et operatio a te semper incipiat, et per te cœpta finiatur.

Omnipotens, sempiterne Deus, qui vivorum dominaris simul et mortuorum, omniumque misereris, quos tuos fide et opere futuros

come, give unto thy servants that peace which the world cannot give; that our hearts being given up to obey thy commandments, and the fear of enemies being taken away, our days, by thy protection, may be peaceful.

Inflame, O Lord, our reins and heart with the fire of the Holy Ghost ; that we may serve thee with a chaste body, and please thee with a clean heart.

O God, the Creator and Redeemer of all the faithful, give to the souls of thy servants departed the remission of all their sins ; that through pious supplications they may obtain the pardon which they have always desired.

Prevent, we beseech thee, O Lord, our actions by thy inspirations, and further them with thy continual help ; that every prayer and work of ours may always begin from thee, and through thee be likewise ended.

Almighty, everlasting God, who hast dominion over the living and the dead, and art merciful to all, who thou foreknowest

esse prænoscis: te supplices exoramus: ut pro quibus effundere preces decrevimus, quosque vel præsens sæculum adhuc in carne retinet, vel futurum jam exutos corpore suscepit, intercedentibus omnibus Sanctis tuis, pietatis tuæ clementia omnium delictorum suorum veniam consequantur. Per Dominum nostrum.

℟. Amen.

will be thine by faith and works; we humbly beseech thee that they for whom we intend to pour forth our prayers, whether this present world still detain them in the flesh, or the world to come hath already received them stripped of their mortal bodies, may, by the grace of thy loving kindness, and by the intercession of all the Saints, obtain the remission of all their

sins. Through thy Son Jesus Christ our Lord, who liveth and reigneth with thee, in the unity of the Holy Spirit, God, for ever and ever. ℟. Amen.

℣. Domine, exaudi orationem meam.

℟. Et clamor meus ad te veniat.

℣. Exaudiat nos omnipotens et misericors Dominus.

℟. Amen.

℣. Et fidelium animæ, per misericordiam Dei, requiescant in pace.

℟. Amen.

℣. O Lord, hear my prayer.

℟. And let my cry come unto thee.

℣. May the almighty and merciful Lord graciously hear us.

℟. Amen.

℣. And may the souls of the faithful, through the mercy of God, rest in peace.

℟. Amen.

Litany of the Blessed Virgin;

COMMONLY CALLED THE LITANY OF LORETTO.

Ant. Sub tuum præsidium confugimus, sancta Dei Genitrix, nostras deprecationes ne despicias in necessitatibus nostris; sed a periculis cunctis libera nos semper, Virgo gloriosa et benedicta.

Ant. We fly to thy patronage, O holy Mother of God, despise not our petitions in our necessities; but deliver us always from all dangers, O glorious and blessed Virgin.

Kyrie eleison. — Lord have mercy.
Kyrie eleison. — *Lord have mercy.*
Christe eleison. — Christ have mercy.
Christe eleison. — *Christ have mercy.*
Kyrie eleison. — Lord have mercy.
Kyrie eleison. — *Lord have mercy.*
Christe audi nos. — Christ hear us.
Christe exaudi nos. — *Christ graciously hear us.*

Pater de cœlis Deus, — God the Father of heaven,
Fili Redemptor mundi Deus, — God the Son, Redeemer of the world,
Spiritus Sancte Deus, — God the Holy Ghost,
Sancta Trinitas, unus Deus, — Holy Trinity, one God,

Miserere nobis. — *Have mercy on us.*

Sancta Maria, — Holy Mary,
Sancta Dei Genitrix, — Holy Mother of God,
Sancta Virgo Virginum, — Holy Virgin of virgins,
Mater Christi, — Mother of Christ,
Mater divinæ gratiæ, — Mother of divine grace,
Mater purissima, — Mother most pure,
Mater castissima, — Mother most chaste,
Mater inviolata, — Mother inviolate,
Mater intemerata, — Mother undefiled,
Mater amabilis, — Mother most amiable,
Mater admirabilis, — Mother most admirable,
Mater Creatoris, — Mother of our Creator,
Mater Salvatoris, — Mother of our Saviour,

Ora pro nobis. — *Pray for us.*

Virgo prudentissima,	Virgin most prudent,
Virgo veneranda,	Virgin most venerable,
Virgo prædicanda,	Virgin most renowned,
Virgo potens,	Virgin most powerful,
Virgo clemens,	Virgin most merciful,
Virgo fidelis,	Virgin most faithful,
Speculum justitiæ,	Mirror of justice,
Sedes sapientiæ,	Seat of Wisdom,
Causa nostræ lætitiæ,	Cause of our joy,
Vas spirituale,	Spiritual Vessel,
Vas honorabile,	Vessel of honour,
Vas insigne devotionis,	Singular Vessel of devotion,
Rosa mystica,	Mystical Rose,
Turris Davidica,	Tower of David,
Turris eburnea,	Tower of ivory,
Domus aurea,	House of gold,
Fœderis arca,	Ark of the covenant,
Janua cœli,	Gate of heaven,
Stella matutina,	Morning star,
Salus infirmorum,	Health of the sick,
Refugium peccatorum,	Refuge of sinners,
Consolatrix afflictorum,	Comforter of the afflicted,
Auxilium Christianorum,	Help of Christians,
Regina Angelorum,	Queen of Angels,
Regina Patriarcharum	Queen of Patriarchs,
Regina Prophetarum,	Queen of Prophets,
Regina Apostolorum,	Queen of Apostles,
Regina Martyrum,	Queen of Martyrs,
Regina Confessorum,	Queen of Confessors,
Regina Virginum,	Queen of Virgins,
Regina Sanctorum omnium,	Queen of all Saints,
Regina sine labe originali concepta,	Queen conceived without original sin,
Agnus Dei, qui tollis peccata mundi,	Lamb of God, who takest away the sins of the world,

Ora pro nobis.

Pray for us.

Parce nobis, Domine.

Agnus Dei, qui tollis peccata mundi,

Exaudi nos, Domine.

Agnus Dei, qui tollis peccata mundi,

Miserere nobis.

Christe audi nos.

Christe exaudi nos.

Ant. Sub tuum præsidium confugimus, sancta Dei Genitrix, nostras deprecationes ne despicias in necessitatibus nostris ; sed a periculis cunctis libera nos semper, Virgo gloriosa et benedicta.

℣. Ora pro nobis, sancta Dei Genitrix.

℟. Ut digni efficiamur promissionibus Christi.

Oremus.

Gratiam tuam, quæsumus, Domine, mentibus nostris infunde : ut qui, Angelo nuntiante, Christi Filii tui Incarnationem cognovimus, per Passionem ✠ ejus et Crucem ad Resurrectionis gloriam perducamur. Per eundem Christum Dominum nostrum.

℟. Amen.

℣. Divinum auxilium maneat semper nobiscum.

℟. Amen.

Spare us, O Lord.

Lamb of God, who takest away the sins of the world,

Graciously hear us, O Lord.

Lamb of God, who takest away the sins of the world,

Have mercy on us.

Christ hear us.

Christ graciously hear us.

Ant. We fly to thy patronage, O holy Mother of God, despise not our petitions in our necessities ; but deliver us always from all dangers, O glorious and blessed Virgin.

℣. Pray for us, O holy Mother of God.

℟. That we may be made worthy of the promises of Christ.

Let us pray.

Pour forth, we beseech thee, O Lord, thy grace into our hearts ; that we, to whom the Incarnation of Christ thy Son was made known by the message of an Angel, may, by his Passion ✠ and Cross, be brought to the glory of his Resurrection. Through the same Christ our Lord.

℟. Amen.

℣. May the divine assistance remain always with us.

℟. Amen.

TE DEUM LAUDAMUS.

Te Deum laudámus : *
te Dóminum confitémur.

Te ætérnum Patrem *
omnis terra venerátur.

Tibi omnes angeli, * tibi
cœli, et univérsæ potes-
tátes :
Tibi chérubim et séra-
phim, * incessábili voce
proclámant :
Sanctus, sanctus, sanc-
tus, * Dóminus Deus Sá-
baoth :
Pleni sunt cœli et terra, *
majestátis glóriæ tuæ.

Te gloriósus * Apostoló-
rum chorus.
Te Prophetárum * lau-
dábilis númerus.

Te Mártyrum candidá-
tus * laudat exércitus.
Te per orbem terrárum *
sancta confitétur Ecclésia.

Patrem * imménsæ ma-
jestátis.
Venerándum tuum ve-
rum * et únicum Filium.
Sanctum quoque * Pará-
clitum Spíritum.

We praise thee, O God :
we acknowledge thee to be
the Lord.
All the earth doth wor-
ship thee : the Father everlasting.
To thee all angels cry
aloud : the heavens and all
the powers therein :
To thee cherubim and
seraphim : continually do
cry :
Holy, holy, holy : Lord
God of Sabaoth.

Heaven and earth are
full : of the majesty of thy
glory.
The glorious choir of the
Apostles : praise thee.
The admirable company
of the Prophets : praise
thee.
The white-robed army of
Martyrs : praise thee.
The Holy Church
throughout all the world :
doth acknowledge thee.
The Father : of an infi-
nite majesty.
Thy adorable, true : and
only Son.
Also the Holy Ghost :
the Comforter.

Tu Rex glóriæ,* Christe.

Tu Patris * sempitérnus es Fílius.

Tu ad liberándum susceptúrus hóminem, * non horruísti Vírginis úterum.

Tu devícto mortis acúleo, * aperuísti credéntibus regna cœlórum.

Tu ad déxteram Dei sedes, * in glória Patris.

Judex créderis * esse ventúrus.

[1] Te ergo quæsumus, tuis fámulis súbveni, * quos pretióso sánguine redemísti.

Ætérna fac cum Sanctis tuis, * in glória numerári.

Salvum fac pópulum tuum, Domine, * et bénedic hæreditáti tuæ.

Et rege eos, et extólle illos, * usque in ætérnum.

Per singulos dies * benedícimus te.

Et laudámus nomen tuum in sæculum, * et in sæculum sæculi.

Dignáre, Dómine, die isto, *sine peccáto nos custodíre.

Thou art the King of Glory : O Christ.

Thou art the everlasting Son : of the Father.

When thou tookest upon thee to deliver man : thou didst not abhor the Virgin's womb.

When thou hadst overcome the sting of death : thou didst open the kingdom of heaven to all believers.

Thou sittest at the right hand of God : in the glory of the Father.

We believe that thou shalt come : to be our Judge.

We pray thee, therefore, help thy servants : whom thou hast redeemed with thy precious blood.

Make them to be numbered with thy Saints : in glory everlasting.

O Lord, save thy people : and bless thine inheritance.

Govern them : and lift them up for ever.

Day by day : we magnify thee.

And we praise thy name for ever : yea, for ever and ever.

Vouchsafe, O Lord, this day : to keep us without sin.

[1] Here it is usual to kneel.

Miserére nostri, Dómine, * miserére nostri.

Fiat misericórdia tua, Dómine, super nos : * quemádmodum sperávimus in te.

In te, Dómine, sperávi; * non confúndar in ætérnum.

O Lord, have mercy upon us : have mercy upon us.

O Lord, let thy mercy be shewed upon us : as we have hoped in thee.

O Lord, in thee have I hoped : let me not be confounded for ever.

On occasions of Thanksgiving the following are added:

℣. Benedictus es, Domine, Deus Patrum nostrorum.

℟. Et laudabilis, et gloriosus in sæcula.

℣. Benedicamus Patrem et Filium, cum Sancto Spiritu.

℟. Laudemus et superexaltemus eum in sæcula.

℣. Benedictus es, Domine Deus, in firmamento cœli.

℟. Et laudabilis, et gloriosus, et superexaltatus in sæcula.

℣. Benedic, anima mea, Dominum.

℟. Et noli oblivisci retributiones ejus.

℣. Domine, exaudi orationem meam.

℟. Et clamor meus ad te veniat.

℣. Dominus vobiscum.

℟. Et cum spiritu tuo.

℣. Blessed art thou, O Lord, the God of our fathers.

℟. And worthy to be praised, and glorious for ever.

℣. Let us bless the Father and the Son, with the Holy Ghost.

℟. Let us praise and magnify him for ever.

℣. Blessed art thou, O Lord, in the firmament of heaven.

℟. And worthy to be praised, glorious and exalted for ever.

℣. Bless the Lord, O my soul.

℟. And forget not all his benefits.

℣. O Lord, hear my prayer.

℟. And let my cry come unto thee.

℣. The Lord be with you.

℟. And with thy spirit.

Oremus.

Deus, cujus misericordiæ non est numerus, et bonitatis infinitus est thesaurus piissimæ majestati tuæ pro collatis donis gratias agimus, tuam semper clementiam exorantes :

Let us pray.

O God, whose mercies are without number, and the treasure of whose goodness is infinite : we render thanks to thy most gracious Majesty for the gifts thou hast bestowed upon us, evermore beseeching thy clemency : that as thou grant-

ut qui petentibus postulata concedis, eosdem non deserens, ad præmia futura disponas.

Deus, qui corda fidelium Sancti Spiritus illustratione docuisti: da nobis in eodem Spiritu recta sapere, et de ejus semper consolatione gaudere.

Deus, qui neminem in te sperantem nimium affligi permittis, sed pium precibus præstas auditum: pro postulationibus nostris, votisque susceptis gratias agimus, te piissime deprecantes, ut a cunctis semper muniamur adversis. Per Christum Dominum nostrum.

Psalm lxxxiii.

Quam dilécta tabernácula tua, Dómine virtútum! * concupíscit et déficit ánima mea in átria Dómini.

Cor meum et caro mea* exultavérunt in Deum vivum.

Etenim passer invénit sibi domum: * et turtur nidum sibi, ubi ponat pullos suos.

Altária tua, Dómine virtútum: * Rex meus, et Deus meus.

Beáti qui hábitant in domo tua, Dómine:* in sæ-cula sæculórum laudábunt te.

est the petitions of them that ask thee, thou wilt never forsake them, but wilt prepare them for the rewards to come.

O God, who hast taught the hearts of the faithful by the light of the Holy Spirit: grant us, by the same Spirit, to have a right judgment in all things, and evermore to rejoice in his consolation.

O God, who sufferest none that hope in thee to be afflicted over much, but dost afford a gracious ear unto their prayers: we render thee thanks for that thou hast heard our supplications and vows; and we most humbly beseech thee, that we may evermore be protected from all adversities. Through Christ our Lord.

Quam dilecta.

1 How lovely are thy tabernacles, O Lord of hosts: my soul longeth and fainteth for the courts of the Lord.

2 My heart and my flesh: have rejoiced in the living God.

3 For the sparrow hath found her a house: and the turtle a nest for herself, where she may lay her young.

4 Even thy altars, O Lord of hosts: my King and my God.

5 Blessed are they that dwell in thy house, O Lord: they shall praise thee for ever and ever.

Beátus vir cujus est aux-
ílium abs te . * ascensiónes
in corde suo dispósuit, in
valle lacrymárum, in loco
quem pósuit.

Etenim benedictiónem
dabit legislátor, ibunt de
virtúte in virtútem : * vi-
débitur Deus deórum in
Sion.

Dómine Deus virtútum,
exaúdi oratiónem meam : *
aúribus pércipe, Deus Jacob.

Protéctor noster áspice,
Deus : * et réspice in fáciem
Christi tui.

Quia mélior est dies una
in átriis tuis * super míllia.

Elégi abjéctus esse in
domo Dei mei, * magis
quam habitáre in tabérná-
culis peccatórum.

Quia misericórdiam, et
veritátem díligit Deus : *
grátiam et glóriam dabit
Dóminus.

Non privábit bonis eos
qui ámbulant in innocéntia:
* Dómine virtútum, beátus
homo qui sperat in te.

6 Blessed is the m
whose help is from the
in his heart he hath di
posed to ascend by ste
in the vale of tears, in t
place that he hath fixed.

7 For the lawgiver sh
give a blessing, they sh
go from virtue to virtu
the God of gods shall
seen in Sion.

8 O Lord God of hos
hear my prayer : give e
O God of Jacob.

9 Behold, O God,
protector : and look u
the face of thine Anoint

10 For one day in t
courts : is better than
thousand.

11 I have chosen rat
to be an abject in the ho
of my God : than to dw
in . the tabernacles of
ners.

12 For God loveth me
and truth : the Lord
give grace and glory.

13 He will not depriv
good things them that w
in innocence : O Lord
hosts, blessed is the m
that hopeth in thee.